This book belongs to

....

QUARTO
Knows

Quarto is the authority on a wide range of topics.

Quarto educates, entertains and enriches the lives of our readers—enthusiasts and lovers of hands-on living.

www.quartoknows.com

© 2019 Quarto Publishing plc

First published in 2019 by QED Publishing, an imprint of The Quarto Group.
The Old Brewery, 6 Blundell Street,
London N7 9BH, United Kingdom.
T (0)20 7700 6700 F (0)20 7700 8066
www.QuartoKnows.com

A catalogue record for this book is available from the British Library.

ISBN 978-1-78603-610-0

Based on the original story by Peter Bently and Duncan Beedle

Author of adapted text: Katie Woolley
Series Editor: Joyce Bentley
Series Designer: Sarah Peden

Manufactured in Dongguan, China TL112018

9 8 7 6 5 4 3 2 1

MIX
Paper from responsible sources
FSC® C104723
www.fsc.org

Reading Gems

Munch Crunch Lunch

Focus sounds in this book

ch
mun**ch**

sh
ship

th (soft)
things

ng
ki**ng**

th (hard)
that

5

The bugs.

I am Nid.

I am San.

I am Gop.

I am Pem.

The bugs are off to lunch with Nid.

Just then some things fell down.

"That is a lot of soft stuff!" said Pem.

Chomp!

Catch!

Splash!

Then there was a big bang!

Crash! Bash! Bump!

"There you are, Nid," said San.

"There are lots of soft things to get rid of," said the bugs.

"Soft things are yum," said Nid
with a big munch!

Then Nid went to his pod.

"My pod is all bent!" he said.

Nid was upset.

The bugs had to help.

Pem got rid of
the pot.

Gop got thick bits
to fix the pod.

San got lots of
thin bits.

But Nid's pod was not fixed.

"My pot is lost!" said Nid.

"Quick!" said Gop.

The bugs get into her ship.
They go to the pond.

20

They get the pot.

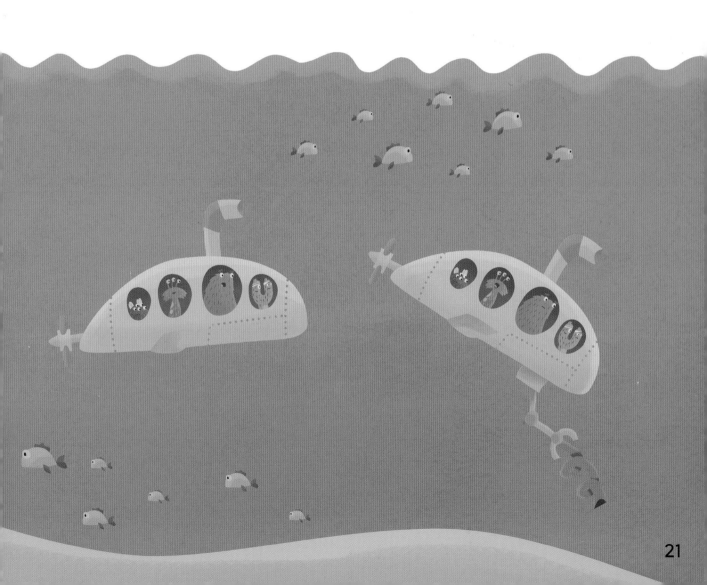

The Munch Crunch King!

"This is my pond!" he said.

The Munch Crunch King was cross with them all!

"Quick, get the ship up!" said San.

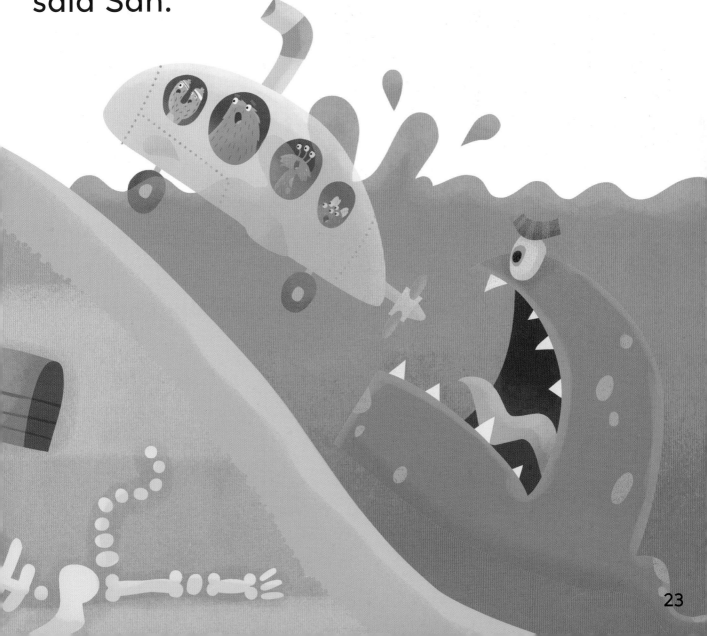

Nid put the pot back on his pod.

Then they all sat down for lunch.

Nid had a stash of soft things!

Munch, crunch, lunch!

Let's Talk About Munch Crunch Lunch

Look at the back cover.

Point to the focus letters.

Can you make the letter sounds?

Can you find the tricky word 'my' in the story?

Point to the letters 'sh' at the start of the word 'ship'.

What sound does 'sh' make?

Can you find some other words in the story with the letters 'sh' in them?

Can you think of any other words with 'sh' in them?

Find the letter 'g' at the beginning of Gop's name.

Can you sound out the whole name?

Can you read all the other bugs' names?

Why was the Munch Crunch King cross?

How did the bugs get back home?

What did the bugs do at the end of the story?

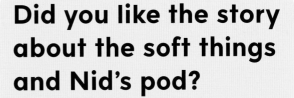

Did you like the story about the soft things and Nid's pod?

What was your favourite bit?

Fun and Games

Look at the letters in the box. Use them to complete some of these words from the story.

ch	sh	th (hard)	th (soft)	ng

ki........

ba........

........ing

........at

lun........

........en

mun........

........in

........ip

........ick

Nid's pod is in a mess. Can you help
Nid unjumble the tricky words by his house?

my   you   they   her   all   are

eyht

ym   rea

ehr

ouy

lal

Reading With Your Little Bugs

Here are some tips to help you enjoy
reading this book with your child.

1 Encourage your child to read the story to you,
   saying the sounds and putting them together
   to read the word.

2 If your child gets stuck on a word,
   show them how to break it down
   into sounds.

3 Have fun! You could make up silly
   voices for each of the characters
   and even act out the story together.

4 Remember to give your child lots
   of praise!

5 If your child is starting to feel tired
   or bored, put the book away
   and pick it up another day.

Have fun and
enjoy reading my
story together.

Mind-Boggling Phonics Glossary

Phonics often feels a bit confusing,
with lots of alien terms. This glossary
will help demystify Phonics!

blend to put individual sounds together to read a word, e.g. s-n-a-p blended together reads 'snap'.

CVC word a word spelled with a consonant, then a vowel, then a consonant, like 'sat' or 'tip'.

decode to put sounds and letters together to read a word correctly.

digraph two letters representing one sound, e.g. ck in 'kick'.

grapheme a letter or group of letters representing one sound, e.g. t, b, sh, ch, igh, ough (as in 'though').

phoneme a single unit of sound, e.g. the letter 't' represents just one sound and the letters 'sh' represent just one sound.

segment to split up a word into its individual phonemes in order to spell, e.g. the word 'cat' has three phonemes: /c/ /a/ /t/.

sight words or high-frequency words are words that appear most often in printed materials. They may not be decodable using phonics (or too advanced) but they are useful to learn separately by sight to develop fluency in reading.

tricky words are words that cannot be sounded out with phonics, such as 'the', 'was' and 'one'. Sometimes called exception words.

trigraph three letters representing one sound, e.g. igh in 'night'.

GET TO KNOW READING GEMS

Reading Gems is a series of books that has been written for children who are learning to read. The books have been created in consultation with a literacy specialist.

The books fit into five levels, with each level getting more challenging as a child's confidence and reading ability grows. The simple text and fun illustrations provide gradual, structured practice of reading. Most importantly, these books are good stories that are fun to read!

Phonics is for children who are learning their letters and sounds. Simple, engaging stories provide gentle phonics practice.

Level 1 is for children who are taking their first steps into reading. Story themes and subjects are familiar to young children, and there is lots of repetition to build reading confidence.

Level 2 is for children who have taken their first reading steps and are becoming readers. Story themes are still familiar but sentences are a bit longer, as children begin to tackle more challenging vocabulary.

Level 3 is for children who are developing as readers. Stories and subjects are varied, and more descriptive words are introduced.

Level 4 is for readers who are rapidly growing in reading confidence and independence. There is less repetition on the page, broader themes are explored and plot lines straddle multiple pages.

Phonics

"There are lots of soft things to get rid of," said the bugs.

"Soft things are yum," said Nid with a big munch!

Simple sentences ✓

Specific sounds and letters ✓

Repeated tricky words ✓

Pictures and words support one another ✓